First published by Parragon in 2010
Parragon
Queen Street House
4 Queen Street
Bath BA1 1HE, UK

ISBN 978-1-4454-1170-5

Printed in China

STORYBOOK COLLECTION

Bath · New York · Singapore · Hong Kong · Cologne · Delhi · Melbourne

TABLE OF CONTENTS

Cinderella

The Heart of a Champion

Life at the palace was a dream come true for Cinderella, and she took care to share her good fortune with everyone she loved. This included her dear old horse, Frou, who had been her faithful friend since she was a child.

One day, Cinderella was visiting Frou in the royal stable when her mouse friends, Jaq and Gus, ran up to tell her that a messenger had arrived at the palace! Cinderella said good-bye to Frou and the other horses, and hurried off to hear the news.

11

Cinderella arrived at the castle just in time to hear the Grand Duke read the invitation aloud: "'Dear King—'" he began.

"That's me!" the King said, beaming.

12

"Quite so," the Grand Duke agreed. "Ahem. 'You and your family,'" he read on, "'are hereby invited to attend this year's annual Royal International Horse Show, to be held exactly one week from today. Please choose one member from your royal household to represent you in the competition.'"

"Whoopie!" exclaimed the King. "I love horse shows. Blue ribbon, here I come!"

"Er . . . you know, Your Majesty," the Grand Duke said, "every year you enter the competition . . . and every year you come in last. Perhaps, just this once, someone else should—"

"Silence!" cried the King. "I have an idea. Every year, I enter the competition. Perhaps, just this once, someone else should represent our kingdom."

"Brilliant, Your Majesty," the Grand Duke said. "I would never have thought of that."

"You know, Father," the Prince spoke up, "there's no finer horsewoman in the kingdom than Cinderella. I think she should represent us."

"Cinderella?" the King said in surprise. He rubbed his chin thoughtfully, then he smiled.

"That," he declared, "is an excellent idea!"

17

The next thing Cinderella knew, the King was leading her out of the palace and back to the royal stable.

"Naturally," he told Cinderella, his voice echoing across the stalls, "the finest horsewoman in the kingdom must have the finest horse in the kingdom. I have a stable full of champions, my dear. We'll choose the best of the best, and you can begin training right away. Ah, yes! I can see those blue ribbons already!"

The King ordered his groomsmen to saddle up his fanciest horses – all one hundred and twenty-two of them – and bring them out to the courtyard for Cinderella to see. Within minutes, there was a row of regal steeds lined up as far as the eye could see.

"Come, Cinderella," the King said, pointing towards the first horse. "Climb on. Don't be shy. You can't know if the shoe fits unless you try it on!"

21

Cinderella climbed onto the back of the first horse. She knew this stallion was one of the King's personal favourites. But he was just a bit too small.

"Too bad," said the King, shaking his head. "Next!"

The next horse, however, was too big. . . .

The one after that wasn't quite right either. . . .

And neither was the next one. . . .

Or the next one!

23

Finally, Cinderella slid down from the saddle of a nervous thoroughbred and dashed back into the stable.

"I'll be right back!" she called to the King, the Prince, and the Grand Duke. "I know the perfect horse! You'll see!"

24

Moments later, Cinderella returned, leading Frou! The old horse was a bit bewildered to find himself on display before the King.

The King stared at Cinderella and Frou in disbelief.

"What's this?" he demanded.

"Why, 'this' is a horse!" Cinderella replied with a laugh. She rubbed Frou's shaggy mane. "The best horse in the kingdom, in fact!"

"My dear," said the King, turning up his nose. "If none of my horses suits your fancy, I can have another hundred champions here by morning!"

"Frou may be old," said Cinderella, "but he has the heart of a champion!" And with that, she saddled Frou and swung herself up.

"Come on, Frou," she told him. "Let's show them what you've got."

But the first thing Frou did was trip over a nearby water trough. Cinderella flew over Frou's head. She landed in the trough with a splash! The other horses whinnied with laughter. Frou hung his head.

"Don't worry," Cinderella said to the King, as well as to Frou. "By next week, we'll be ready."

Every day for a week, Cinderella and Frou trained for hours. But Frou kept making mistakes.

No matter how sweetly Cinderella urged him, he missed every jump.

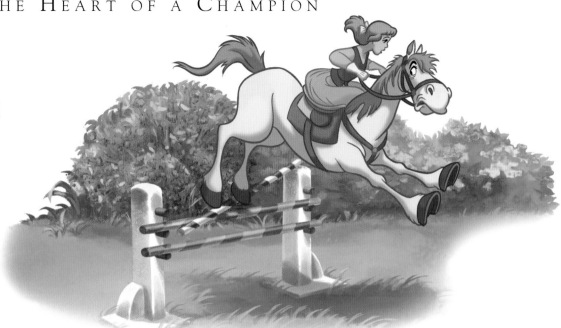

And no matter how firmly she steered him, he took the wrong turn every time.

"Oh, Frou," Cinderella said, patting his shaggy head, "I know you can do it!"

But no one else was quite so sure – especially not Frou!

33

At last, it was the night before the royal horse show.

"Please don't worry," Cinderella told Frou. "You're going to be wonderful. Tomorrow will be fun!" But Frou didn't seem to believe her.

"Did someone say 'fun'?" a voice asked. Cinderella turned around. It was her Fairy Godmother!

"I overheard your little mouse friends talking," she explained. "They said you need a miracle. So, here I am!"

Cinderella laughed and shook her head. "Oh, that's kind of you," she said. "But we don't need a miracle, just a good night's sleep."

"My dear," her Fairy Godmother whispered, "you know Frou can win, and I know Frou can win, but our friend Frou doesn't know it at all. What he needs is a reason to feel confident."

And with that, she raised her magic wand and waved it at Frou. To Frou's amazement, a glass horseshoe appeared on each of his hooves!

"With these horseshoes, you'll never miss a step," she told Frou, sneaking a wink at Cinderella. "And while I'm at it," she added, "Bibbidi-Bobbidi-Boo!" She waved her wand again. Instantly, a golden saddle appeared on Frou's back, and Cinderella's simple dress became a beautiful riding habit.

"How can we ever thank you?" asked Cinderella.

"As you said," replied her Fairy Godmother, "just have fun!"

The next day at the horse show, Cinderella saw more fine horses than she ever had before. They all looked like champions – but so did Frou! He held his head up high and stamped his hooves proudly. The King himself could hardly believe that Frou was the same horse he'd been watching trip and stumble all week long.

Frou cleared every jump with ease and never took an awkward step or a wrong turn. He even managed a graceful little bow at the end. And it was all thanks to the magical glass horseshoes – or so Frou thought.

Cinderella knew better, though. The glass horseshoes just gave Frou the confidence he needed in order to be the great horse he always had been.

In the end, there was no question about who belonged in the winner's circle.

"First place goes to Princess Cinderella and Frou!" declared the judge. The Prince took Cinderella's hand and gently kissed it. "I knew you'd win," he told her.

Cinderella smiled at Frou. "And I knew you'd win," she said.

"You know," the King told the Grand Duke, "I had a special feeling about that horse all along. . . ."

41

After the horse show, Frou returned to his stall at the palace stable, with his head a little higher, his back a little straighter, and his glass shoes at the ready for the next time duty called.

Snow White
and the Seven Dwarfs

To the Rescue

Snow White and her prince spent nearly every day together. But one particularly sunny morning, the Prince told Snow White that he had an important errand to take care of. "I will be away for several hours, I'm afraid," he said.

"I'll miss you," said Snow White. She herself was planning on spending the day in the palace gardens.

Snow White changed her dress and set about her gardening. The Prince saddled his trusty steed, Astor, and rode to the garden to bid Snow White farewell.

"Take good care of my prince," Snow White said, slipping a flower into Astor's bridle.

Then she gave one to the Prince. "And take good care of Astor!" she said. (For Snow White loved the faithful horse, too.) She smiled and waved as she watched them trot off down the road.

The time flew by. Before long, Snow White looked up from the roses she was tending and saw a cloud of dust on the road. A horse was rapidly approaching.

"Oh, good!" she exclaimed, clapping her hands together. "The Prince and Astor are home early!"

Brushing the dirt from her clothes, she hurried towards the gate to greet them as they arrived.

Imagine Snow White's surprise when she saw that Astor was alone!
The Princess looked from Astor's empty saddle to the now quiet road.
"Why, where's the Prince?" she wondered out loud.
But only Astor knew the answer, and, of course, the horse couldn't say.

Snow White tried not to panic. But her tender heart quickly filled with dread.

Surely the Prince is in some sort of trouble, she thought. Why else would Astor return to the palace without him?

"I must go and find him!" she declared bravely. And without wasting another moment, she grabbed her cloak and started down the road.

Suddenly, Snow White felt a warm breath on the back of her neck. She turned – and there was Astor. "What is it?" she asked.

The horse stamped her hoof on the ground and nodded towards her empty saddle.

"Do you want me to get on?" Snow White asked. Again, Astor nodded.

Goodness! thought Snow White. Maybe she can tell me where the Prince is, after all! Quickly, the Princess pulled herself into the saddle. She barely had time to sit down before Astor was racing down the road towards the forest!

57

Astor ran deeper and deeper into the woods with Snow White tugging uselessly at the reins. The Princess tried not to think about what dangers might await them on the dark path ahead.

If only she knew where Astor was taking her. If only she knew that the Prince was safe!

Tirelessly, Astor galloped through the woods. She darted between trees and leaped over briars and brambles. Then, suddenly, Snow White spotted a piece of red cloth caught on a long, sharp thorn.

A knot formed in her throat. Could it be? It was! A scrap torn from the Prince's very own riding cloak!

And that wasn't all! As she ducked beneath a low-hanging branch, Snow White glimpsed a spot of red on the muddy ground. There was no mistaking those deep crimson petals. They were from the very rose Snow White had given the Prince that morning!

She tugged on Astor's reins, begging the horse to stop. But Astor charged ahead, and Snow White had no choice but to go along.

At last, they reached the river. Surely Astor will have to stop here, Snow White thought. But the pace only quickened. Indeed, it was soon clear to Snow White that Astor planned to jump across the river!

Just then, Snow White saw the Prince's feathered hat dangling from a limb high above the water.

There was no time to think. As Astor leaped across
the river, Snow White reached up as high as she could
... and plucked the hat from the branch.

65

Snow White gripped Astor's reins with one hand. With
the other, she clutched the Prince's hat to her chest. She could only
imagine the horrible danger her dear, sweet prince was in.
Her thoughts were soon interrupted by a startling noise.
Four eyes glared at her from the shadows ahead.
"Oh!" Snow White cried. Astor bravely reared up to defend her.

"Well, tello hair . . . I mean, hello there!" said a familiar voice.

"Doc?" Snow White said, with a sigh of relief. "I'm so very glad to see you!"

"Likewise, my dear. But what's the matter?" Doc asked, surprised to see the Princess looking so upset.

"It's the Prince," Snow White said, showing him the crumpled hat. "I have to find him!"

"Don't worry, Princess," Doc assured her. "We can help you!"

Doc put his fingers to his lips and whistled. Within seconds, the other Dwarfs arrived.

"The Prince is missin'," Doc explained to the Dwarfs. "And we're gonna help Snow White find him!"

"Let's . . . let's . . . let's – achoo! – let's go!" Sneezy cried.

"Oh, thank you," Snow White said as Astor impatiently stamped her hooves. "Just follow Astor," she added. "She seems to know the way."

71

The Seven Dwarfs and their ponies followed Snow White and Astor through the depths of the forest and over a deep, rocky canyon.

"Ooh," said Bashful, looking down. "I hope the Prince isn't down there."
"Shh!" Grumpy growled back at him. "You'll scare the Princess."
But Snow White had heard. She clutched the Prince's hat and concentrated on thinking hopeful thoughts.

Finally, they emerged into a sunny clearing, and Astor slowed to a stop.

Snow White blinked in the bright light and then spotted the Prince, lying on the ground. "Oh, no!" she cried.

Astor knelt down slightly so the Princess could slip out of the saddle. The faithful horse whinnied as Snow White ran to the Prince's side.

"Don't worry!" Snow White called to the Prince as she raced across the clearing. "I'm coming!"

Breathless, Snow White reached the Prince just as he sat up and stretched. "What a nice nap!" he said. "And what a lovely way to awake. I hope you're hungry!"

Snow White was bewildered. Next to the Prince lay a lavish picnic spread out on a soft blanket. And the Prince was as happy and healthy as ever!

"I knew Astor would get you here quickly," he said, beaming. "Tell me. Are you surprised?"

Snow White paused for a moment to catch her breath.

"Oh, yes, very surprised," she said at last, smiling.

The Prince looked amused as the Seven Dwarfs began digging into the delicious food.

"Well," he said with a laugh, "I'm glad I brought a little extra."

"Me, too," Snow White replied. She picked up an apple and offered it to Astor. "And," she added, "I'm very glad you have such a dear and clever horse!"

79

Beauty and the Beast

A Friend for Phillipe

It was a beautiful, sunny morning when Belle arrived at Phillipe's stable with a special surprise for her friend.

"Guess what I have!" she called happily as she hurried to his stall. "The first carrots of the season, Phillipe! I picked them just for you!"

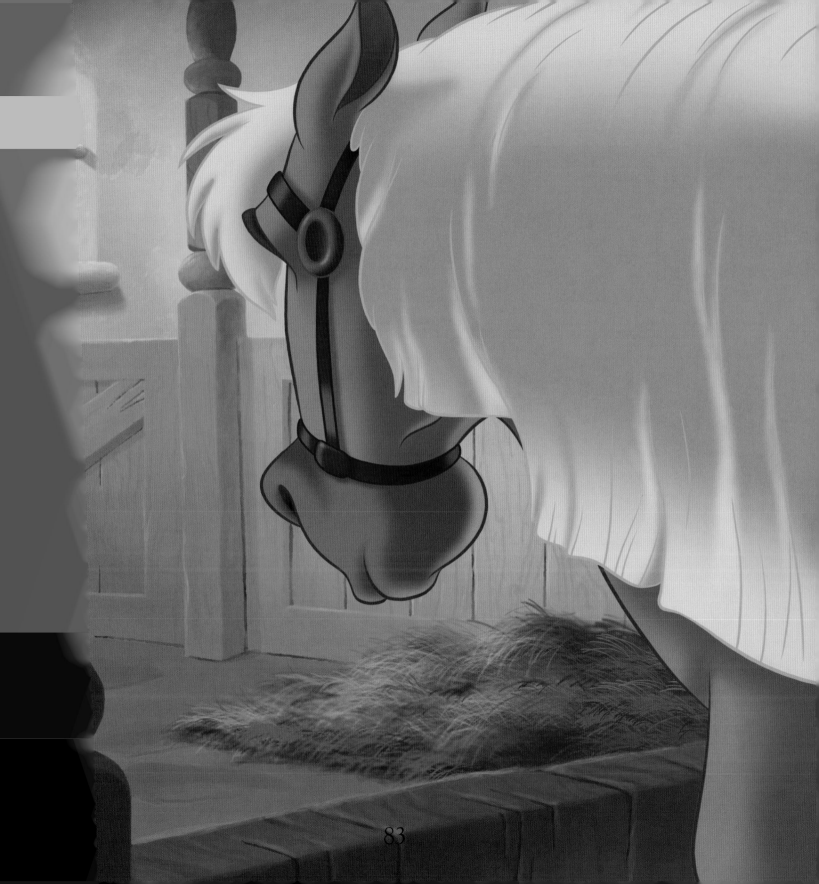

Phillipe was not as happy as Belle had hoped he would be. He sniffed at the bunch of carrots. But when Belle offered him one, Phillipe gently butted her hands away.

"Is something wrong?" Belle asked, alarmed. Phillipe was always hungry.

Phillipe hung his head and sighed a little sigh. There was something wrong, all right, Belle thought. Phillipe was the gloomiest horse she had ever seen!

Belle decided that she simply had to cheer up Phillipe. But how?

"If only you could talk," Belle said to Phillipe, "you could tell me exactly what to do." But he couldn't, so Belle would have to work it out on her own. She hurried to the library and gathered all the books about horses she could find. Then she sat down to read every single one of them.

Carrot Soup
for the
Horse's Soul

Horses
Who Love Oats
Too Much

"Sacre bleu!" cried Lumiere when he, Cogsworth, and Chip saw all the books. "What are you doing, Princess?"

"I want to cheer up Phillipe," Belle explained. "I hoped I'd find the answer in one of these books . . . but I'm not having much luck."

"Ah!" said Lumiere, "before you came and freed us from the enchantment, we were often sad."

"But," the former candelabrum remembered, "we always found ways to cheer ourselves up. You must brighten his stall! It's important to have the right atmosphere, you know!"

"I do believe that music is the key to happiness," Cogsworth said. "It always made me smile when I was an enchanted clock."

"Or how about a bubble bath?" Chip chimed in. "That used to cheer me up!"

89

Belle decided to give each idea a try.

First, she helped Lumiere brighten up Phillipe's stall. They covered the walls with wallpaper and trimmed them with gold. They piled pillows in the corners, hung curtains in the windows, and filled the room with flowers. And for the final brightening touch, they hung a huge chandelier from the ceiling.

"Voilà!" Lumiere exclaimed. "What more could a horse ask for?"

Phillipe stared sadly out the window.

"I wish I knew," said Belle.

Next, Cogsworth set up an orchestra in the stable. Belle, Lumiere, and Chip listened politely as Cogsworth led the musicians through a very, very long concert.

Phillipe didn't seem to enjoy the concert much at all. But at least, Belle thought brightly, his appetite has returned!

Finally, Belle saw to it that Phillipe was treated to a bubble bath fit for a king. "If this doesn't make him smile," Belle told Chip, "I don't know what will!"

But in the end, though he was shiny and sweet-smelling, Phillipe was just as glum – and Belle was just as puzzled.

"Maybe the Prince will know what to do," Chip suggested.

94

Belle thought this was an excellent idea. She found the Prince in his study and explained everything to him. "I wish I knew what Phillipe needed!" she cried. "Do you have any suggestions?"

The Prince thought for a moment. "Maybe a walk would do him good," he said. "A good walk always used to cheer me up."

"Of course!" Belle agreed. "That's a wonderful idea!"

Quickly, Belle changed into her riding clothes and hurried to fetch Phillipe's saddle. When he saw her coming, he perked right up.

"Silly me! What was I thinking?" Belle said as she saddled him. "You'd really like a nice ramble, wouldn't you?"

Belle led Phillipe to the edge of the forest where the royal orchards began. The sight of all of the delicious fruit gave Belle an idea.

"Would you like an apple?" Belle asked. "Go ahead and choose one!"

Following Belle's suggestion, Phillipe wandered from tree to tree, eyeing each apple and even sniffing some. But soon his head was hanging, and his steps were slow and heavy. It was clear his heart wasn't in it.

Still, Belle did not give up. They continued on to a wide, open meadow.

"You know," Belle said, "I bet a good gallop would do the trick." She leaned forward and snapped the reins, giving Phillipe's sides a firm nudge with her heels.

As if to tell her, "Wrong again," Phillipe stopped, leaned down, and nibbled at the clover.

"Oh, Phillipe," Belle said in despair. "I just don't know what else to do!"

Then, all of a sudden, Phillipe's ears pricked up, and his head snapped to attention. Belle barely had time to sit up before Phillipe charged off like a racehorse out of the gate!

"Whoa, boy!" Belle cried, nearly falling out of the saddle. "Phillipe! Where are you going?"

But Phillipe just charged on, straight into the forest.

A FRIEND FOR PHILLIPE

At last they emerged from the trees . . . into a clearing filled with wild, beautiful horses! Belle and Phillipe stared at the herd before them. Then Phillipe whinnied, and several of the wild horses answered him.

Finally, Belle realized what Phillipe had wanted. Not a fancy stall, or fine music, or a bubble bath. Not an apple or a run. What Phillipe had wanted was to be with other horses!

"Well, go on," Belle said as she swung out of the saddle. "Go have some fun!"
She didn't have to tell him twice. Phillipe trotted eagerly over to the herd.
All afternoon, Belle watched Phillipe race and play. Soon, he had even made
a friend! The two horses grazed, chased each other around the clearing, and dozed
together in the warm sun.

All too quickly, the day was over, and the sun began to set.

"Oh, goodness!" cried Belle. "We've got to get going!"

So she put Phillipe's saddle on and they started back towards the castle. "I promise we'll come back soon!" Belle told Phillipe.

As they made their way through the meadow, Belle found herself wishing Phillipe had a horse friend at the castle. "If only there was a way—" Belle began.

She was interrupted by the sound of hooves behind them. Belle turned around.

"Well, look at that, Phillipe!" she exclaimed. "It's your new friend."

The horse who had played with Phillipe all afternoon was following them home.

Belle and Phillipe slowed their pace, and the shy horse drew closer . . .

. . . and closer.

By the time they reached the castle, the two horses were walking side by side.

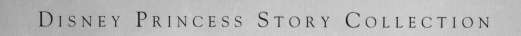

"Welcome to our castle!" Belle told the new horse when they arrived. "We're honored to have you as our guest!"

And to show the horse she meant it, Belle hurried to fix up the stall next to Phillipe's.

"There," she said when she was finished. "Now this looks like a stable where a horse (or two!) could really live happily ever after!"

And that is exactly what they did.

Sleeping Beauty

Falling in Love

Once upon a time, in a faraway land, there lived a king and queen. They longed to have a child and, after years of waiting, their wish was granted.

A daughter was born. They named her Aurora after the dawn, because she filled their life with sunshine.

To celebrate her birth, the King and Queen declared a holiday. Guests travelled from near and far to visit the tiny Princess, including three good fairies called Flora, Fauna and Merryweather. Each fairy would bless the Princess with a single, magical gift. Flora blessed the child with beauty. Fauna gave the gift of song. But before Merryweather could cast her spell, a gust of wind blew through the great hall.

In a flash of lightning, a tall, dark figure appeared. It was the evil fairy Maleficent, who was furious that she hadn't been invited to the party.

"I too, have a gift to bestow on the child," she said with a wicked grin. "Before the sun sets on her sixteenth birthday, she shall prick her finger on the spindle of a spinning wheel and die!" With that, she disappeared in a burst of foul green smoke.

The King and Queen were panic-stricken. Flora tried to calm them. "Don't despair," she said. "Merryweather still has her gift to give."

Although her magic was not strong enough to undo the curse, Merryweather did have the power to help.

And so, with a wave of her magic wand, Merryweather declared, "Not in death, but just in sleep the fateful prophecy you'll keep. From this slumber you shall wake, when True Love's Kiss the spell shall break."

Still, the fairies thought, perhaps there was an even better way to save the Princess from the curse. What if they pretended to be peasant women and raised the Princess as their own in a secret, far-off place for sixteen years? If Maleficent could not find Aurora, how could she harm her?

FALLING IN LOVE

The King and Queen sadly agreed to the plan, knowing it was the only way they could protect their daughter from Maleficent. They watched with heavy hearts as the fairies changed themselves into humans and disappeared into the night with the Princess.

By morning, the fairies and the Princess arrived at an old cottage deep in the woods, which became their home. The fairies stopped using magic and pretended to be Aurora's aunts. They called her Briar Rose, so that no one would learn of her whereabouts. That would keep her safe from Maleficent.

The years passed quickly and before they knew it, Briar Rose's sixteenth birthday had arrived. To celebrate, the fairies planned a surprise – they would make the girl a beautiful dress and a delicious cake! But first they had to get her out of the cottage. So they sent her to pick berries.

Briar Rose enjoyed strolling through the woods. As she walked, she sang to the forest animals who had become her friends, all the time dreaming of a tall, handsome prince.

Little did she know that a real prince just happened to be riding through the forest that very morning.

"Hear that?" the Prince said to his horse, Samson. The sound of Briar Rose's sweet voice had drifted over to him. The Prince was enchanted – he had to find out where it was coming from!

Eagerly, he urged his horse into a gallop – but as Samson leaped over a log, the Prince fell off. He landed in a creek with a most undignified splash.

"No carrots for you!" he scolded as he climbed out of the water. He laid his hat, cape and boots out to dry. At the same time, he couldn't help but wonder about the voice that he'd heard. It was almost too beautiful to be real.

"Maybe it was some mysterious being," he said, "a wood sprite, or a – " But his thoughts were interrupted by the shocking sight of his wet clothes beginning to fly and hop away. Briar Rose's animal friends were stealing them!

"Why, it's my dream prince!" Briar Rose laughingly declared when the rabbits and birds appeared before her, dressed in the stolen clothes. "You know, I'm really not supposed to speak to strangers, but we have met before." And while the real Prince looked on, hidden behind a nearby tree, Briar Rose began to sing and dance with her dressed-up forest friends.

As Briar Rose turned away, the real Prince quickly stepped in. When he began to sing with her, she spun around.

"Oh!" she gasped.

Her three aunts were always warning her to stay away from strangers … and yet there was something so familiar about this young man (whom she never dreamed was an actual prince). She couldn't help but feel that they had met before.

Long into the afternoon, Briar Rose and the Prince sang and danced together and before either one could help it, they had fallen in love.

When Briar Rose finally returned to the surprise party that awaited her at the cottage, it was her aunts who were most surprised.

"This is the happiest day of my life," Briar Rose said with a sigh. Then she told them about the young man she'd just met and how she'd invited him to the cottage that very evening.

"This is terrible," moaned Flora. "You must never see that young man again." She explained to Briar Rose that she was already betrothed – and had been since birth – to a young prince called Phillip.

"But how could I marry a prince?" Briar Rose asked. "I'd have to be . . ."

". . . a princess," Merryweather finished.

The fairies then told Briar Rose about her real parents and her real name. Flora, Fauna and Merryweather changed themselves back into fairies, wrapped the Princess in a cloak and set off for the palace immediately.

They arrived at the castle just as the sun began to set. The poor Princess was so sad about not being able to see the young man from the forest again that the fairies left her for a moment so she could collect herself. As soon as they were gone, a wisp of green smoke appeared and lured Aurora up a tower to a hidden room.

Slowly, the smoke took the form of a spindle and Maleficent's voice filled the air. "Touch the spindle!" she ordered. Aurora pricked her finger on the spinning wheel and fell into a deep sleep. The only thing that could save her was True Love's Kiss.

Unfortunately, Maleficent had locked the Prince in her dungeon. The good fairies found him and discovered that he was Prince Phillip, the same Prince who was betrothed to Aurora! They gave him enchanted weapons with which to fight Maleficent. Though the evil fairy changed herself into a fierce dragon, she was no match for the Prince's bravery – or the magic sword and shield. He soon defeated her.

Prince Phillip raced to the palace and knelt beside the Sleeping Beauty. Ever so gently, he kissed her on the lips. He sighed with relief as she opened her eyes and smiled at him.

136

FALLING IN LOVE

Soon, a grand, joyous wedding was announced. True love had conquered all!

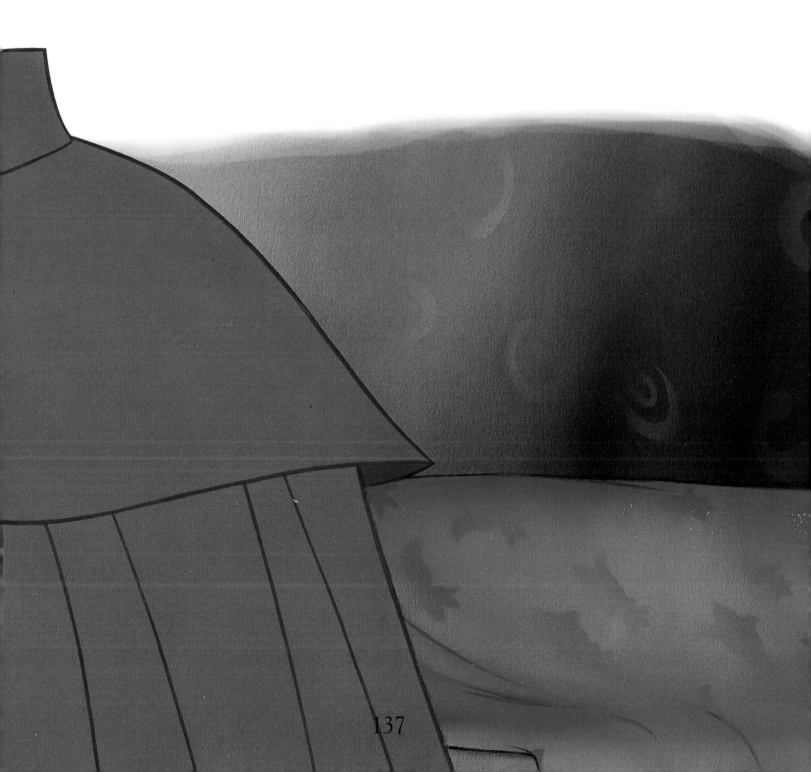

The Princess Who Didn't Want to Marry

Princess Jasmine giggled at her pet tiger, Rajah, as she sat by the fountain in the palace courtyard. The tiger had not been impressed with the latest Prince to ask for Jasmine's hand in marriage, so he'd helped scare him away. They were both glad to be rid of the selfish suitor, one of many unworthy princes who'd visited recently.

Jasmine's father, the Sultan of Agrabah, was not amused. "Dearest, you've got to stop rejecting every suitor who comes to call," he told his daughter. "The law says you must be married to a prince by your next birthday. You've only got three more days!"

Jasmine thought that the law was unfair. "Father, I hate being forced into this," she said. "If I do marry, I want it to be for love."

Lately she'd found herself wishing she weren't a princess at all. She had never even been allowed to go outside the palace walls. She felt trapped.

That night, the Princess decided to run away. She put on a disguise and began to climb over the palace wall. Rajah tugged on her dress – he didn't want her to leave.

Jasmine knew she would miss her friend, but she had to see what else was out there.

"I'm sorry, Rajah, but I can't stay here and have my life lived for me," she explained.

Rajah nodded and slid his head under Jasmine's foot to give her a boost over the wall.

The next morning, Jasmine arrived at the marketplace. She looked around excitedly, for she had never seen anything like it. People were selling everything from pots and necklaces to fish and figs. As she walked, she came upon a little boy who looked like he hadn't eaten in a while.

"Oh, you must be hungry," Jasmine said. The boy looked up at her eagerly. She took an apple from a nearby stand and handed it to the poor child.

"You'd better be able to pay for that," the apple seller said.

"Pay?" Jasmine said with surprise. She'd never needed to pay for anything at the palace.

"No one steals from my cart!" the vendor bellowed and grabbed her angrily. Jasmine was frightened and didn't know what to do.

Luckily, a handsome stranger came to her rescue.

"Oh, thank you, kind sir," the young man said to the apple seller. "I'm so glad you found her. I've been looking all over."

Jasmine looked puzzled. "What are you doing?" she whispered to the young man. She noticed that he had a pet monkey with him.

"Just play along," he replied.

"You know this girl?" the seller asked him.

"Sadly, yes. She is my sister," he replied. "She's a little crazy. She thinks the monkey is the Sultan."

Jasmine knelt down. "Oh, wise Sultan," she said to the monkey, "how may I serve you?"

"Tragic, isn't it?" the young man said as Jasmine pretended to be crazy. "Now come along, sis. Time to go see the doctor."

They started to leave. It looked like they would escape until the monkey bowed good-bye . . . and a bunch of stolen apples tumbled from his vest!

"Come back here, you little thieves!" the fruit seller yelled. The trio ran as quickly as they could and finally reached the young man's rooftop home. They were safe … for now.

Jasmine looked around. The stranger's home was simple, but at least it was his own. No one told him what to do. Jasmine couldn't imagine having so much freedom.

At the same time, the young man was looking longingly at the palace in the distance. It would be wonderful to live there, he thought, to have enough money so he wouldn't have to worry about his next meal.

"Sometimes I just feel so trapped," they both said.

Surprised, they looked at each other. Jasmine suddenly felt that she had a lot in common with this handsome stranger. But just then, angry palace guards burst in. Jasmine looked around – there was no escape!

"Do you trust me?" asked the young man, holding out his hand to her. She looked into his brown eyes and said, "Yes."

"Then, jump!" he cried.

Jasmine took his hand and they leaped off of the roof. They landed safely in a pile of grain, then raced through the marketplace . . . right into another set of guards!

The head guard seized the young man. It's the dungeon for you, boy!" he declared.

"Unhand him!" demanded Jasmine, pulling down her hood and revealing herself as the Princess. The guard was shocked to see her outside the palace walls. "Do as I command," she ordered. "Release him."

"I would, Princess, except my orders come from Jafar," the guard replied. "You'll have to take it up with him."

Jasmine crossed her arms and narrowed her eyes. "Believe me, I will," she said.

Back at the palace, the Princess confronted Jafar, one of her father's advisors. The evil man told her that the stranger had been sentenced to death and killed.

"I am exceedingly sorry, Princess," Jafar lied.

149

Jasmine glared at Jafar. "How could you?" she said and ran out. She went to see her tiger friend. "It's all my fault, Rajah," she said, sobbing. "I didn't even know his name."

The next day, on the streets of Agrabah, there was a magnificent parade. Men playing drums marched down the street, followed by women dancing with scarves. All of the townspeople stopped what they were doing to watch.

Inside the palace, the Sultan heard the music. He went to his balcony and was delighted by what he saw below. "Oh, Jafar!" he called. "You must come and see this!"

Reluctantly, Jafar joined the Sultan.

Trumpets blared and banners waved as the parade made its way to the palace. But most impressive was Prince Ali, who sat on top of an enormous elephant, throwing gold coins into the crowd. He looked attractive, regal – and extremely smug.

Princess Jasmine, who was still upset about the death of the young man from the market, watched from her balcony. She shook her head in disgust at this latest suitor. Did he think he could buy her hand in marriage?

Nevertheless, the Sultan welcomed Prince Ali into the palace.

"Your Majesty, I have journeyed from afar to seek your daughter's hand," said Prince Ali after flying in on a magic carpet.

"Prince Ali Ababwa," said the Sultan, "I'm delighted to meet you."

But Jafar had his own sneaky plan: he wanted to marry the Princess himself so that someday he would rule the kingdom. He whispered to the Sultan, "What makes him think he is worthy of the Princess?"

Confidently, Prince Ali replied, "Just let her meet me. I'll win your daughter."

But Jasmine had been listening and was very upset. "How dare you – all of you! Standing around deciding my future," she cried. "I am not a prize to be won!" She turned and stormed off.

But Prince Ali would not give up. That evening, he appeared on Jasmine's balcony and apologized. Rajah growled protectively and was about to chase him away, but Jasmine thought the Prince looked familiar. When she stepped closer, he offered to take her on a magic carpet ride.

"We could get out of the palace . . . see the world," Prince Ali offered.

Jasmine hesitated. "Is it safe?" she asked, looking at the carpet.

Prince Ali leaned forwards, offering his hand. "Do you trust me?" he asked. Jasmine thought he might be the young man from the marketplace!

Maybe he hadn't been killed, after all! She gave him her hand and climbed aboard the Magic Carpet.

Jasmine and Prince Ali flew over the streets and rooftops of Agrabah. They held hands and Jasmine felt happier than ever before.

Jasmine got the Prince to admit that he was the young man from the marketplace. But he didn't tell her everything because he didn't think she would like him if she knew the truth. His real name was Aladdin. After escaping from the dungeon, he'd found a magic lamp. The Genie inside had given him three wishes.

Aladdin, who had fallen in love with Jasmine, had used one of them to become a prince so he could marry her.

"I sometimes dress as a commoner to escape the pressures of palace life," he lied. "But I really am a prince."

"Why didn't you just tell me?" asked Jasmine.

"Well, you know, uh, royalty going out into the city in disguise . . . it sounds a little strange, don't you think?" he said.

Jasmine looked down. "Not that strange," she said quietly.

Soon after they returned from the romantic magic carpet ride, Jafar discovered Prince Ali's secret and revealed his true identity. Then Jafar tried to seize power, but Aladdin and Jasmine fought him bravely and won. Together, they had saved the kingdom.

After the battle, Aladdin took Jasmine's hands in his. "I'm sorry I lied to you about being a prince," he said humbly.

Jasmine held his hands. She hadn't fallen in love with him because she thought he was a prince. She loved him for who he was inside. The Princess had finally found someone she wanted to marry. Her father gladly changed the law so that she'd be able to.

Aladdin and Jasmine climbed aboard the Magic Carpet and kissed. Beneath them was a whole new world where they would live together, happily ever after.